The Essence Of Dreams

Edited By Wendy Laws

First published in Great Britain in 2024 by:

Young Writers
Remus House
Coltsfoot Drive
Peterborough
PE2 9BF
Telephone: 01733 890066
Website: www.youngwriters.co.uk

All Rights Reserved
Book Design by Ashley Janson
© Copyright Contributors 2024
Softback ISBN 978-1-83565-569-6
Printed and bound in the UK by BookPrintingUK
Website: www.bookprintinguk.com
YB0597F

FOREWORD

Welcome Reader, to a world of dreams.

For Young Writers' latest competition, we asked our writers to dig deep into their imagination and create a poem that paints a picture of what they dream of, whether it's a make-believe world full of wonder or their aspirations for the future.

The result is this collection of fantastic poetic verse that covers a whole host of different topics. Let your mind fly away with the fairies to explore the sweet joy of candy lands, join in with a game of fantasy football, or you may even catch a glimpse of a unicorn or another mythical creature. Beware though, because even dreamland has dark corners, so you may turn a page and walk into a nightmare!

Whereas the majority of our writers chose to stick to a free verse style, others gave themselves the challenge of other techniques such as acrostics and rhyming couplets.

Each piece in this collection shows the writers' dedication and imagination – we truly believe that seeing their work in print gives them a well-deserved boost of pride, and inspires them to keep writing, so we hope to see more of their work in the future!

CONTENTS

Aspull Holy Family RC Primary School, New Springs

Sienna Rose (7)	1
Oakley Sherrington (7)	2
Lily Joyce (8)	4
Paige Smith (7)	5
Alex Stewart (7)	6
Ellouise Horrocks (8)	7
Isla Cooper	8
Liam Prince (7)	9
Joshua Prince (7)	10

Bryn Deri Primary School, Castle View Estate

Edward (9)	11
Elsa Sanchez Thomas (9)	12
Alex Williams (10)	14
Oliver Williams (11)	16
Poppy Williams (11)	17
Clara Watkins (11)	18
Tomos Chamberlain (11)	19
Ayla Rogers (9)	20
Daisy Tingle (9)	21
Jack Harvey (10)	22
Amelia (10)	23
Alice Davies (10)	24
Evie Davies (10)	25
Maxwell Graham (9)	26
Louisa Grubb	27
Holly (10)	28
Charlie Wickers (10)	29
S'varra Amruth (10)	30
Mali Titshall (11)	32
Izabella Davies (10)	33

Finlay Greatrex (10)	34
Gryff Medlicott (10)	35

Fox Covert Primary School, Edinburgh

Nitya Ketinedi (10)	36
Elliott Campbell (10)	38
Alex Geary (10)	40
Hugh Short (10)	42
Max Steele (9)	44
Alfie Allan (10)	46
Anna Nisbet (11)	48
Leo Bryce (11)	50
Alara Duman (11)	52
Alice Morrison (10)	54
Emily Ruthven (10)	55
Hana Lam (10)	56
Olivia Kerr (9)	58
Rohan Bullock (11)	59
Hannah Winton (10)	60
Henry Haldane (10)	62
Rory Macdonald (10)	64
Alice Costley (10)	65
Lucas Grant (10)	66
Casey-Rose Mitchell (10)	68
Abby Boyack (10)	69
Emily M (10)	70
Awa Jallow (10)	71
Luke Jenkinson (10)	72
Alba Maiden (10)	73
Cora McRitchie (10)	74
Archie Fraser (10)	76
Theo Daly (10)	77
Ella Miller (11)	78
Zahraa Al-Behadili (10)	79

Edward Quinn (11)	80
Lylah Gilchrist (10)	81
Luke MacKenzie (10)	82
Iona Taylor-Bell (10)	84
Harris Lauchlan (11)	85
Aaron Gault (11)	86
Mark Rusakov (10)	87

Higher Lane Primary School, Manchester

Harriet (10)	88
Priya (10)	90
Inaaya Ishaq (7)	92
Oliver Ware (9)	93
Mila Pearson (10)	94
Gerry Campbell (9)	95
Phoebe Liu (8)	96
Oded (10)	97
Niamh Edney (11)	98
Hayden Newman (7)	99
Alexa Griffiths (11)	100
Lily Boyd (9)	101
Sophia Samaei (7)	102
Ruby Hepburn (7)	103
Matthew Pritchard (9)	104

Holy Family RC Primary School, Oldham

Sherelle-Kay Ngah (11)	105
Zina Aghaunor (10)	106
Princess Manson (10)	107
Nathaniel Warburton (11)	108
Kacper Gorgosz (10)	109
Lilah-Rae Ward (10)	110
Joachim Osaigbovo (10)	111
Ethan Shaw (10)	112
Lexi-Mai Coop (10)	113
Jamison Hufton (11)	114
Aariz Shakeel (10)	115
Madison Ward (10)	116
Kamen Smith (11)	117
Bernice Cardoso (10)	118

Alexander Jones (10)	119
Henzo Da Silva (10)	120
Charlton Saopa (10)	121
Iliana Kara (10)	122
Scarlett Ordano (11)	123
Corey Ashton-Barker (10)	124
Kayla Ogbeide (10)	125
Connor McQuaide (10)	126
Rorey Tindall (10)	127

Kirby Moor School, Brampton

Aaron Devine (11)	128
Andrew Thompson (10)	129

Oak Wood Secondary School, Nuneaton

Riley Fowler	130

Tetherdown Primary School, Haringey

Benjamin O'Dea (9)	131
Grace Lewis (10)	132
Flossie O'Dea (10)	136
Leo Konstantin (11)	138
Paloma Lockwood (9)	140
Isabella Quirke (11)	142
Edie Hearn (10)	144
Zara Zerdoudi (9)	146
Aksel Akdogan (8)	148
Theo Ogden (11)	150
Alma Lanzin Sohar (8)	152
Max Davies (9)	154
Mack Lawrence (9)	155
Cian Styles (10)	156
Alexander Pearce (8)	157
Gabriel Vasiliou (9)	158
Mei-Lei Lerman (10)	160
Nia Hadjinikolova (10)	161
B H (10)	162
Oscar Black (9)	163
Warza Ahmed (9)	164

Esther Mitting (10)	165
Ben Cox (11)	166
Zaki Copnall (8)	167
Emily Fox (9)	168
Annabel Bartlett (9)	169
Olivia Nilsson (10)	170
Amelia Farmer (9)	171
Lottie Hilton (10)	172
Adriell Sitepu (8)	173
Zoe Brick (8)	174
Ben Schonfeld (10)	175
Sophie Bradstock-Smith (10)	176
George Towers (8)	177
Amelia Salgado (8)	178
Jackson Humphries (10)	179
Emily Quirke (7)	180

The Richard Crosse (CE) Primary School, Kings Bromley

Samuel Kirven (8)	181
Ava De Costa (8)	182
Eleanor Parry (9)	184

THE POEMS

A Lonely Flower

I am a flower.
My stem stands tall but my petals are weak.
I am so attractive, the bees come to me.
The sun shines bright on me and that's how I grow.
I may seem pretty but there's something you don't know.
I am separate from all the other flowers, on the lawn my hours are so lonely.
I wait night until dawn and I wait and I wait where could he be?
Where is he, my friend Buzzy Buzzy Bee?
He's finally here, I see him flying high.
When he comes I am so happy and I no longer sigh.
He stays with me and we talk all day,
When he goes I want him to stay, it's okay.
Tomorrow is a brand-new day, it's not the end, he'll be back tomorrow,
Because he is my best friend.

Sienna Rose (7)
Aspull Holy Family RC Primary School, New Springs

Space

Once upon a dream, I was in an egg and it was a space egg
I saw it starting to crack and you always see a snack at the bottom
I felt a funny tummy feeling
I sneezed and there were butterflies in my tummy
And then I saw a crying fairy but she wasn't very scary
So I went up to her, she had a teddy bear and curls in her hair
I asked her what was wrong and her tears were long
She said my wand was broken so I gave it a little poke
It was fixed but a bit mixed
She said, "Oh thank you"
She said, "It's so true"
Suddenly I blasted and lasted over hours crashing to Earth
It was worth
Oh what a wonderful day
I went in a home
Now I said bye to her and realised I can fly
I love this day
And I feel like a dove
I'll come back for sure

I just needed a door.
I put on my cute suit
My egg sock
I was ready to go back to home.

Oakley Sherrington (7)
Aspull Holy Family RC Primary School, New Springs

Astronaut

A ppeared in space, what a sight, on a
S upersonic spaceship zooming through the night.
T ravelling around the moon.
R ight around the constellations, *zoom, zoom, zoom*.
O nwards through the Milky Way turning left and right.
N avigating Neptune, it's shining so bright.
A steroids in my path, "Oh no, what should I do?"
U ranus I spot, it won't be an issue.
T he edge of the solar system is a great place to be... but my belly is rumbling so let's go home for tea.

Lily Joyce (8)
Aspull Holy Family RC Primary School, New Springs

The Tooth Fairy

A light and airy fluttering fairy,
The Tooth Fairy is her name.
Gliding gracefully beneath the moon,
Finding fallen teeth is her aim.
Slipping softly between the sheets,
Fairy dust lights her path.
She's careful not to wake the child,
With twinkly bells or laughs.
Placing a milk tooth in her pocket,
She taps with her wand three times.
Leaving behind a silver coin,
She flits through the window blinds
And off she goes back to Fairy Land.

Paige Smith (7)
Aspull Holy Family RC Primary School, New Springs

The Train Poem

When I wake up and switch on my brain,
My imagination only thinks of trains.
They're super fast, like a bullet from a gun,
They transport you around to look for some fun.
Some are short, but others are longer
Freight trains are cool and much, much stronger.
Virgin trains were red, now Avanti trains are blue,
I love travelling on trains and I think you would too!
So grab a ticket or 2, 3 or more,
And have the best ever 2024!

Alex Stewart (7)
Aspull Holy Family RC Primary School, New Springs

Potter's Poem

The most famous wizard of all is Harry Potter
He went to Hogwarts School
With wizards and witches
Catching golden snitches
He saved them all from Voldemort's rule.

The sorting hat chose the house of Gryffindor
There he met his friends
They flew on broomsticks
Ran through walls made of bricks
And together that's how the war ends.

Ellouise Horrocks (8)
Aspull Holy Family RC Primary School, New Springs

Best Friends

Best friends are the family that you choose.
The loveliest people who you never want to lose.
They always go the extra mile and try their best to make you smile.
Best friends are forever, they are there whenever.
I love my best friend with all my heart.
To the moon and all around the stars.
The only thing you want is a best friend.

Isla Cooper
Aspull Holy Family RC Primary School, New Springs

A Scary Dragon

Dragon, dragon flying high,
Up, up, up in the sky.
He shoots fire out of his mouth
As hot as the sun.
Oh, a scary dragon.

Liam Prince (7)
Aspull Holy Family RC Primary School, New Springs

A Silly Clown

Silly, silly, silly clown,
Always falling down.
Doing his silly tricks,
Juggling with his building bricks.
I love my silly clown.

Joshua Prince (7)
Aspull Holy Family RC Primary School, New Springs

Squishmallow Land

I dream of walking in a path of squishmallows, it was really bright,
It was so bright that everything appeared bright white.
As I step on the floor it squishes
Just like the air when it whooshes.

The air smelt like sweets,
And the squishmallows feel like squishy treats,
They are extremely colourful,
The colours were so delightful.

I jumped on the squishmallows in the dark,
I felt like I was bouncing in a trampoline park,
I bounced, floated, dived and fell,
Looking up it appeared that I had fallen into a well.

At the bottom of the well, I found an escape,
To a room of squishmallows of all different shapes,
Everything in this room was a hobby I like,
From football to gaming consoles and a bike.

I played with the football and scored a goal,
Behind the goal, I saw a hole,
So I jumped in it and it took me back to the well,
I heard a noise but it was only my alarm bell.

Edward (9)
Bryn Deri Primary School, Castle View Estate

My Dream With A Dragon

I slowly walked along the old tracks
Emerged horrifying creatures, from small cracks
Splinters punctured my sore feet
And worst of all, the unbearable heat.

Alas in my sight
A glittering doorway of light
Eerie feelings crowded my mind
This was a bad idea, I would find.

I reached out, to touch the light
It was pulling me, dragging me like a furious kite
A cold, horrible sensation flooded my mind
"Help! Help!" I cried.

I was falling, falling through time and space
Dizzy memories and feelings whizzed past my face
Planets floated, looking tranquil in the meadow of black
In these memories, I saw darkness, fight and attack.

Suddenly, my falling stopped
I had landed, how had I been dropped?
Where I was the floor was bouncy and soft
But I smelt it, I spluttered and coughed.

The awful stench of rotting meat
Cheese and socks and smelly feet
I see in the distance
I walked towards the smell with resistance.

That's where the smell came from
With green scales that shone
Big, dirty claws that dug in the ground
It roared with the sound of a huge crowd.

He stomped towards me
He stretched his tail, as long as a tree
Smashing, crashing and his smell was horrible
Though he did stink, he was formidable.

He stared at me, with large, yellow eyes
His teeth ablaze and covered in flies
His breath smelled like toxic waste
I started to run but he chased.

I tripped and struggled as I tried to flee
I was horrified to realise... he ate me!
My mother woke me from my terrible dream
I don't think things were how they seemed...

Elsa Sanchez Thomas (9)
Bryn Deri Primary School, Castle View Estate

Time

Robo and I
Travel through space and time
In our cosmic spaceship,
We could travel as fast as a whip!
When we were visiting home, our ship had a malfunction,
We teleported to a rocky old destroyed planet,
I tried to stop the ship but it didn't work, we crash-landed!
Into the destroyed lifeless planet we go,
The ground around the spaceship shivered,
The creaky old door opened,
A large puff of dust flew into the air as we set foot on the planet.
Something doesn't feel right about this planet.
We were being watched by an unknown creature,
Hiding in the shadows waiting to make its next move.
Blood-red eyes stared at my soul,
Me and Robo ran like lightning back to the spaceship,
A 10-foot beast chased me as Robo fixed the ship,

Robo's arms went flying in a desperate attempt to fix our ship.
The door closed just in time,
We flew back home to safety and we never saw the beast again.

Alex Williams (10)
Bryn Deri Primary School, Castle View Estate

Flying Royalty

As I sank into my bed my dream began.
Millions of twinkling stars shimmering in the black blanket of sky.
I saw something in the distance that had rocks the size of planets that shone as bright as the sun.
As it came into focus I saw aliens the size of mountains.
As slimy as a slithering snake.
I glided slowly over to the planet.
Beams of bright lights danced through the cold air
Like diamonds waiting patiently in the mines.
I arrived on the mysterious planet, the temperature dropped dramatically.
I spotted lush emerald grass swaying in the cold breeze.
There was a humongous Colosseum.
As I entered the Colosseum the atmosphere was extraordinary.
The Colosseum was shivering and the crowd was roaring.
There were aliens playing the drums intensely
And some aliens were singing proudly.
Bang! I woke up.

Oliver Williams (11)
Bryn Deri Primary School, Castle View Estate

Mythical Stars In The Night Sky

A wonderful atmosphere exploring the dancing solar systems.
My favourite outstanding football player Ella Toone appearing through the distance.
Spectacular stars shining like beautiful turquoise diamonds upon the moon.
Hearing loud rockets crashing, banging and zooming like a lion
Sunlight going down as stars come out.
It felt like an amazing upside-down world in real life, it was like we were so close to the magical stars and moon.
Looking closely, I could see millions of giant black holes on the moon as well as different planets.
There it stood, the whispering star walking down to come and speak to us
One by one they come and talk to us as well as whisper.
Why was that I wonder?
Then I suddenly see a familiar face on another planet with her horse called Strawberry
That's enough for now, perhaps next year...

Poppy Williams (11)
Bryn Deri Primary School, Castle View Estate

Unnamed Planets

Everywhere floats unnamed planets,
Stars glistening in the silent sky,
We canter delicately around a massive Olympic arena,
I can just hear my horse's hooves echo as they hit the sandy surface,
Zero limits apply.

The air tastes so sweet,
Like strawberries on a lively summer's day,
All the planets glow with mysterious colours,
Flickers of sparkle beaming out,
Glaring at me.

No other feeling apart from joy runs through my veins,
Nothing around me has ever been seen by the human eye before,
Every sound I hear is followed by a hollow echo.

We begin to cool down and come back to a gentle walk,
Silence surrounds us,
No one else here,
The stars grow darker,
Everything goes dim,
Apart from the unnamed planets hovering above our heads.

Clara Watkins (11)
Bryn Deri Primary School, Castle View Estate

On The Verge Of Life

Drifting through dark, isolated space,
Pacing planets and awakening asteroids.
Travelling towards an aimless goal,
Towards a blazing universe.
Zooming past celestial supernovas,
The galaxy mouths called my name from black holes.
Stenches from gas planets heaving their weight,
Stars are like roads of angels.
Magnificent meteors manipulated the sun,
Blocking its extended arms.
A burial ground of rockets,
Each is an old NASA project.
Clouds of dust and gas blocked the way,
I would not leave in dismay.
Thick clumps of horrible gas and dust,
Finally, a way past.
A new god-worthy universe,
Planets made of stone, iron and gold.
Bright stars painted stories in the sky,
Tiny worlds of molten magma whizzed by.
A new universe on the verge of life.

Tomos Chamberlain (11)
Bryn Deri Primary School, Castle View Estate

The Olympics

My dream starts on a running track
With my team
Me and my brother have the Olympics in a week
I am a bit nervous
Another day passed of training
Having to train seven hours a day.

Every four years the Olympics come around
Soon as I stepped foot in the Olympics
I could see all my coaches in the stadium
My family were all clapping when I came in
I could see the trophy waving at me and I smiled.

My brother is on the track
I have to get ready for my race
My brother's race starts in five minutes, my family is hyping him up
I shout, "Come on, Charlie!"
Charlie loves running and so do I.

Charlie has started his race
My family shout. "Come on, Charlie!
Go on Charlie." He is in 1st place so far
"Come on Charlie, two more laps"
Me and my brother both came first.

Ayla Rogers (9)
Bryn Deri Primary School, Castle View Estate

Danger Encloses On The Wild

He stares at them with his devilish eyes,
His claws dig into the rocky boulders cries
The cave rumbles and grumbles like a hungry child
A sense of danger encloses the wild.

He has wings as long as a ship's sails
And hard rock like emerald scales
A tail that looks like tug-of-war ropes
That comes along with feet good for slipping down slopes.

A symbol of fear crosses the wild's face
As the beast continues his wild goose chase
He whizzes past the wise old oak trees
And runs through the forest with ease.

He drags the mammals back to his cave-like dome
They have an unexpected party where the wild gets to roam
The sight of two unimaginable enemies having fun
Until the end of the setting sun.

Daisy Tingle (9)
Bryn Deri Primary School, Castle View Estate

Teleporting Into A New Space

One boring and dull day,
As the sand blows into my eyes,
I see the sunset rising.
It was like I splashed paint on a canvas.
I could see some stunning colours.
Such as red, orange and yellow.
But as the sunset dances over me,
I see a deep dark cave.
I crept further towards the miserable cave.
As I got closer I heard some sort of weird voice.
I entered the cave and the noises got closer.
The cave was as dark as a hole in the ground.
But then the unexpected happened, I saw a tall emerald.
It was coming in and out of a portal.
I had built up the braveness to enter the portal,
I teleported onto the moon.
As I walked further,
I suddenly fell through a hole!
But then I opened my eyes and I was in my bed.

Jack Harvey (10)
Bryn Deri Primary School, Castle View Estate

The Space Cat

As I walk onto the runways,
I'm very excited like always.
I marched through the doors as proud as I can be,
The spaceship drifted off into space and I was drinking my warm tea.

I turned around and I saw my furry ginger cat,
I jumped and out of nowhere there was a giant splat,
As I looked out of the window I was in shock,
It was another cat that went, chit-chat.

We just landed on Planet Mars, it was a magical space,
Something dropped and it hurt my face,
It was a bit of rock that was weird,
Boom, it disappeared.

I went into my spaceship happy to fly back,
I put my yummy snacks in my sack,
I went for lift-off and I forgot my clever cat,
This is how my cat became the amazing Space Cat.

Amelia (10)
Bryn Deri Primary School, Castle View Estate

My Dream

In my dream,
Shining stars winking whilst the moon spins.
I'm dancing on Saturn's massive, light brown ring.
The man on the moon gives me a big friendly grin.
The first man on the moon confidently puts the flag on the moon.
Then the sun lets out a big yawn.
Aliens were dancing.
Venus is as bright as a gold coin.
Jupiter was waving to Mercury.
Space dust was slowly disappearing.
Dreamland is full of stars.
I'm floating into the Milky Way
The sight is amazing, there are mixed pinky-brown stars in my sight.
Bang, pieces of star, a star scatters everywhere.
I start to feel frightened!
I woke up, I realised it was in my dream.

Alice Davies (10)
Bryn Deri Primary School, Castle View Estate

Exploring Space

I am in space, how did I get here I wonder?
I look at the wonders of space
And it looks so sophisticated and beautiful.
I look at the glimmering stars.

Floating like a ball for a little bit,
Then I set off like a zooming rocket.
Soon I can see a green bush planet.
I reach down to touch it very slowly and gently.
It was as smooth and bushy as a beaming dog.

My little, small feet are on the ground.
Who are you, little green men?
Suddenly, I hear an astonishingly loud noise.
I quickly realised it was the little green man's friends.

I ran as fast as lightning and jumped like a rabbit.
I floated like a ball in space again.

Evie Davies (10)
Bryn Deri Primary School, Castle View Estate

Underpants' Dream

In my dream, I woke up in the morning to go to school
I got my last pair of pants out of the drawer as swiftly as I quivered
Then suddenly whoosh, my pants flew away like a butterfly
Into a tree as tranquil as a streaming river.

I told my grandad who was doing the washing
He said a new pair would be ready when I got home at four and a half
So, I slowly strolled to school, with no pants on
All my friends laughed as I was feeling embarrassed as if I was a chimpanzee.

When it was home time my grandad said the
Pants vanished and we needed to go to the tree
We fetched a ladder as we sprinted
Me and my grandad got the pants back safe on my bum.

Maxwell Graham (9)
Bryn Deri Primary School, Castle View Estate

If I Was An Astronaut

If I was an astronaut how would I feel?
Floating like I'm a tiny black dot
Sense of pride just like Neil
What an amazing chance I've got!

If I was an astronaut what would I see?
Colourful planets dancing into the dark
My shiny reflection staring back at me
Bombing comets and meteoroids causing a spark

If I was an astronaut what would I touch?
I'd hope to catch a twinkling shooting star in my hands
You can't touch very much
The strange textures feel different to our lands

If I was an astronaut what would I hear?
The muffled voices of hopeful friends back at base
My first step on the moon I hear them proudly cheer
Mission accomplished, landed in space!

Louisa Grubb
Bryn Deri Primary School, Castle View Estate

Ice Skating Dreams

My dream starts when I am putting on my skates,
Feeling excited being with my mates,
Whilst being in a famous ice rink,
Wearing white skates and my jumper that's pink.

We were skating around doing tricks,
Also, the music was a remix,
We were happy and made up dances and routines,
Plus we were all wearing jeans.

At 3pm we came off the ice for food,
But one of my friends was in a mood,
After that, we went on the ice,
I gave my friends some skating advice.

At 5pm we came off the ice,
Skating with my friends was very nice,
Our time together was splendid,
But a few seconds later my dream sadly ended.

Holly (10)
Bryn Deri Primary School, Castle View Estate

Banana Mars

I just left Earth in a banana plane
When I left there was a lot of rain
When I was cruising in the air
Sitting in a comfy chair.

Listening to my favourite song
While playing ping pong
I zoom past a pear planet
I see someone called Janet.

I went past Orange Land
Saw an orange band
I land on Banana Mars
See a lot of banana stars.

I see banana creatures
They have sticky-uppy features
Do you want to dance?
Sure, do you like France?

Charlie Wickers (10)
Bryn Deri Primary School, Castle View Estate

My Dream Of Singing

I had a dream.
I wanted to be supreme.
At that moment I was on stage.
That was on my favourite page.
My time to shine.

People were cheering around a door, people were peering
And waving their arms.
My family were there with love in their eyes.
My time to shine.

I felt so nervous but at the same time, I felt so proud.
The audience was definitely wowed.
I sang my famous song.
All my fans were cheering along.
My time to shine.

How did I come here?
I forgot I was having so much fun.
When my performance was over we went to the back.
Then *boom*, it was all black.
My time to shine.

I went to the back
As my alarm woke me up from my dream
I was as sad as rain.

S'varra Amruth (10)
Bryn Deri Primary School, Castle View Estate

The Whispering Planet And I

In my dreams every night
I fly above to my desire
There it stood
The whispering star
I peeked over the gorgeous fireball
And there it was... Saturn
With a circle of stars around its creamy ring
Shimmering waves with some hints of bling
It whispers to me in complete silence
It's like it tells me to float away to another land
Next stop...
The scorching moon in space
With an emerald star that stays.

Mali Titshall (11)
Bryn Deri Primary School, Castle View Estate

Vegetable Planet

Sophie and I shoot off to the sky.
In a long carrot rocket, its nose is flying high.
Our rocket carrot whizzed by, past a potato planet with a dirty face.
We are so excited to see a potato in space.
As we continued to explore we saw a broccoli munching a rock.
A broccoli alien, that's such a shock.
We pick blueberry stars from the sky to eat on our journey home.

Izabella Davies (10)
Bryn Deri Primary School, Castle View Estate

The Helicopter Dream

I dream of flying over the gorgeous Red Sea
Piloting a helicopter as big and beautiful as can be
The dog was sitting in the back for free
He was brown, white and black, glowing with glee.

We start descending from the sky
Having fun on this magnificent ride
Coming down from up high
Coming into shore following the tide.

Finlay Greatrex (10)
Bryn Deri Primary School, Castle View Estate

Cotton Candy Clouds

Cotton candy clouds,
They fill the world with joy.

The planes plough through the clouds,
And everyone enjoys.

Everyone overcrowds the airport to get a candy jet,
Filled with cats, dogs, astronauts and cowboys.

Trust me there's not a threat
You really would enjoy.

Gryff Medlicott (10)
Bryn Deri Primary School, Castle View Estate

The Raccoon Revolution

There was once a thriving community of people
There were kids playing and food getting stolen by seagulls
But the raccoons had enough of being called a pest
They decided to take the world, now they have a quest

Step by step they slowly take America
They take Brazil, India and even Nigeria
Oh look they have reached the deep ocean to begin their dive
They hated it but they knew when they finished they would thrive

They have now taken the world
And stolen every beautiful pearl
They will now steal everything
And show off their bling-bling

The raccoons are seeking revenge
The humans will have regret
As the raccoons avenge
They will get slaves using threat

As the humans hide
The raccoons thrive

Boom, boom, boom went the raccoons' feet
The humans accept defeat

They are now getting jobs
Police, astronauts and even some rob
They are now in search of distant planets
But before they can go they need food, they check the tubs, tins and cabinets

They zoom to an unknown planet, unaware of what they're up against
They land on a planet called Monkey and start up their defence
Suddenly they get attacked by cheeky monkeys which is very intense
They zoom back to Earth in fear and very tense

Now they shall choose their ruler
They have to make a decision
Or they have to fight
The option is very tight

They have chosen the mighty one
The raccoons have really won.

Nitya Ketinedi (10)
Fox Covert Primary School, Edinburgh

Monkey Mania

When the monkeys came that dreadful night,
It gave me quite a bit more than a fright.
On that dreadful night.
They distracted the guard by throwing a big blue shoe
And escaped from the zoo with so much to do!
They got their pitchforks and their knives,
They got their signs saying, 'We will save monkey lives!'
On that dreadful night.
They stole a golf cart from a store,
They rode it till the sun began to snore.
From zoo to zoo they threw the big blue shoe,
To distract the guard and let the monkeys get through!
On that dreadful night.
As the riot became larger,
The human's fight for freedom became harder.
As the population diminished,
We were well and truly finished.
On that dreadful night.
The monkeys were powerful but we were strong,
We didn't stop fighting until we were done.
The end was near and so was our fear,
Until they took over the animals, our greatest peers.
On that dreadful night.

That was the moment we realised we failed,
We surrendered to the monkeys as the human race began to fade...
Stomp, stomp, stomp went the monkeys' feet,
As we had to admit defeat.
On that dreadful night.
They captured us all apart from me,
Although I was grateful I didn't have much glee.
"Hey!" the monkey said as he got up from his bed,
"You're the guy who threw the big blue shoe into the original zoo!
We can't capture you."

Elliott Campbell (10)
Fox Covert Primary School, Edinburgh

President Dexter

My big strong cat Dexter Geary,
He is going to take over the world.
I have a very weird theory,
That my cat is hurling
The world to victory.
I woke up one night,
In Washington D.C,
To see my cat president,
With the Secret Meow (the Secret Service)
And he is trying to jump,
Onto the meowidential podium,
To make meow laws,
The secret meow gets a cat crane,
To help him on the podium
He's on the podium,
He has fallen and the Secret Meow puts him back on the large podium,
He is saying *meow*, "All food for cats so we live with luxury."
Meow. "No more water, kitty milk, milkshakes and whiskey."
Meow. "We will have humans as protection against the dogs!"

Meow, meow, meow. "That's meowidential speech over, goodbye."
He walks behind him to fall off again with a crash and a very loud *meow!*
And walks out with his cat suit in a bit of a scruff but okay,
Just then about 100 ambulances arrived and 100 police escort officers arrived too,
And fixed up Dexter even though nothing was wrong
And then a warning *meow* and *fffff* came from him,
The dream is almost over, it's coming to an end,
The dream will now stop, it's 8:15, school is coming.

Alex Geary (10)
Fox Covert Primary School, Edinburgh

Sweet Kingdom

In the dead of night, you sometimes get a fright
But in a dream so light it's bound to be very bright
A place where your worries fade away
And somewhere you can play and play!

In a world full of sweetness it's like heaven but better
The swoosh of the waves getting you wetter and wetter
And when you catch the guinea pig tram
It will run across the tracks but it does not take lambs.

The next stop is Sweet Kingdom
Where all the walls are made from chocolate, there's so much freedom
And rivers of Fanta that flow free
Who wouldn't want to be me?

To the left a dancing cat
But to the right, you have DJ Pig who plays on a mat
For we are coming up to a football game
Filled to the brim with a surfing chihuahua who has a lot of fame
Guinea pig golf, *whack!* See the ball spin
For playing it gives you quite a grin.

For on the tram, it's watermelon galore
Watermelon juice, give me more.

The last stop is Sweet Kingdom we're almost there
At last, it's time for me to meet the mayor
At last, we arrived
What's that?
All our friends are here, we met on the journey!

But at last a dream so good always has to end.

Hugh Short (10)
Fox Covert Primary School, Edinburgh

Once Upon A Dream

Once upon a dream
My eyes see a beam
As fast as I can go I rush into my house
Oh no I see a mouse in my house
But something scared it
Feared it.

Then I saw my door I saw a shadow
It wasn't my shadow and I went to see what it was
A mouse, I tried to catch it, it was as fast as a cheetah
But it was faster than someone in a cast because it was too fast
Sneakily I went up the creaky stairs.

I heard a loud bang! I screamed!
I need to be really quiet.
I go to my room I look out my window
Into my street, there is a house for sale.

I don't remember a house being for sale
Then the lights turned on, I was shocked
How is someone in there if it is for sale
No one broke into the house
I see a mouse, again I let it run.

I just needed to focus on the house,
I tried to go to sleep but I couldn't,
I was so worried about the house
I looked again but the lights were off
I panicked, oh no I heard a
Knock on my door

What should I do? I am not going to answer it because
I don't know who it is
I look out my window
No one is there...

Max Steele (9)
Fox Covert Primary School, Edinburgh

The Football Champs

In the changing room, we were nervous
The coach was nervous too
You could hear the football boots clashing
Our kit is super bright blue.

I am the captain and at the front
I have to do most of the work
They scored a goal we were giving up
And I remembered I am fast
And scored a goal
"Alfie, Alfie," the football fans screamed, "Alfie is the best,"
Everyone's face was as red as a tomato, thankfully we were not last.

2-2 I scored another goal.
"Yessss, half-time," the whistle blows.
"We can do this, this is tough," said Alfie
And the players said, "Here we go."
Second half starts, one of the players injured his leg,
We were one man down, all of the players were nervous and beg.

Here comes the final penalty shoot-out, *dun, dun, dun*
We scored one goal, "Yessss," they missed - yes this is fun

And if I miss they would still be in the game - here comes Alfie, he dinks
"Yessss." We have won the cup and in the changing room he drinks.

Alfie Allan (10)
Fox Covert Primary School, Edinburgh

The Lorax And Me

As I realised where I was
My head finally stopped spinning
I sat down and started chilling
Then a little house sat there
Way off in the vast distance
And there I saw a man
Who sat there doing some fishing
He was orange and very short
And spoke for all the trees
And he had some knobbly knees
His name was the Honourable Lorax
And he would set the trees free
As I slowly approached him
His expression turned to unmistakable glee
His eyes were full of kindness
And he was staring at me
He was orange like a pumpkin
And full of lots of cheer
He had a very bushy moustache
And I knew I shouldn't fear
He flickered his sweet little eyelashes
And then he shed a tear
Most of the trees were ash

We don't need all this paper
It will help if you remember
Remember all the trees that died
The ones that turned to ember
So now I have to glide
Now that the story is done
I really do have to run
I am stuck in this dream
Just the Honourable Lorax and me.

Anna Nisbet (11)
Fox Covert Primary School, Edinburgh

Sweetie Land

One day I stumbled into a big turquoise crystal portal
For about a minute I was only staring at nothingness - I was feeling really chortle
A minute went by, I popped out onto a big spongy cake
I knew that this was a big mistake
That minute I began to ache but then
I realised that this was my dream
Then a big beam of light shone in my eye
Oh no, there were dry gingerbread men - it was a big supply
There were about ten, I thought, *this isn't a bad idea*
There was a load of candy canes and jelly tots
And lots of spots of marshmallows and lollipops
I started eating some very good sweets
A few minutes later it felt like I ate a whole street!
I made friends with the gingerbread men - we ate jelly tots
Little did I know it was their evil little plot!
They were planning to capture me
But I knew karate
And I would turn them into a patty

I ate their arms and legs
After I finished every last crumb
Now it's time I'm done!

Leo Bryce (11)
Fox Covert Primary School, Edinburgh

The Nightmares

They come in the night as soon as your head hits the pillow
They make you scream till you cry and all you see is black
All you can do is look back, no pink milk only black and white
Maybe blood, it feels like you can't move or speak
No sparks in the sky
Just scream like you can't breathe, they hold your breath
Till you can't breathe and then they let go before you pass
They torture you, trying to move but you can't
These nightmares are getting out of control

You grow up with them, they know you better than you know you
You might think not but I know they are like your dark friend
Don't scream out like Halloween - rats and hats in the sky
But then you hear creaking - it's a black shadow
Then you scream but by the time it gets to you, you disappear

Into the clouds, you lift your head and it's black, you think you're trapped
But you realise you are in your room and it's time for breakfast.

Alara Duman (11)
Fox Covert Primary School, Edinburgh

The White Lady

Inside my head when I'm lying in my bed
Dreams, nightmares who knows what's said?
A door appears in front of me
Should I enter? It's up to ye
A big shadow appears, coming towards
Okay I'll enter the door
The shadow is as big as a ski resort
I've got to go through the door no doubt
"Who are you, why are you here?"
"I'm a ghost I live near."
"Help me get home, please."
"Okay, I won't tease."
"What's your name, White Lady?"
"Okay let's go, my friend."
In the living room, there is a baby
Well, it's a spider baby or well a blended one.
"This is not my home,
I need to go back to my universe."
Wow that was fast, now I've got a comb
I'm going in my house now, bye to my family.
That's one of my dreams, there are many more...
Inside my head when I'm lying in my bed!

Alice Morrison (10)
Fox Covert Primary School, Edinburgh

The Cursed Forest

The night came and everyone in the house fell asleep
Alba was almost asleep when she heard a beep
She didn't think much about it so she ignored it
After about two minutes she fell asleep for a bit

In her dream, she was in a dark forest with reeds
Everywhere she stepped there were weeds
She went exploring in caves
But when she went in them they looked like waves

She was trying to find her home but she saw a person
It looked like it was shapeshifting, but she wasn't certain
It started to come closer to her
She thought it was about to eat her, but came out a small purr

It brushed itself against her, but she fell to the floor
But blood came to pour, pour, pour but there was more, more, more
It was now morning, her mum came to wake her up
But she didn't wake up till her mum heard someone say sup!

Emily Ruthven (10)
Fox Covert Primary School, Edinburgh

Once Upon A Dream

What's in my mind when I'm lying in bed?
A flying dog, my own flying dog
Cute paws standing on your lap waiting for a pat
Woof! Woof! My dog barked as impatient as a four-year-old
Angel wings flapping upon your ceiling
With a little waggy tail
Adorableness you can't resist.

Where would I go in my dreamland?
My eyes opened and I saw a unicorn, I was surprised
Luckily I understand it's not evil
And it even offered me a cotton candy
I don't want to leave, the dream is too wonderful to be awakened in this dream
Just then I saw a stream
Where a team of beautiful unicorns appear.

The team of unicorns had a
Long rainbow mane and glittery hooves
White skin as clean as a whistle.

I turned around and saw another unicorn
I tried to ride it but it was gone

I looked upon
Where the sky lay
I guess it's the end of my dream.

Hana Lam (10)
Fox Covert Primary School, Edinburgh

My Most Vivid Bad Dream

Me, my sister, my friend and her brother
Went to climb a mountain just us and no other
We want to try and get to the summit
And we want to try not to plummet
We walked and we walked until we reached our goal
But then we realised the mountain was going to fall
We ran and we ran as fast as we could
And when we reached the bottom, we fell down like planks of wood
We lay there for ages until all was quiet
And then we heard an enormous riot
Bang, crash, rumble
The mountain began to shake
As violently as an earthquake!
There it was again
Bang, crash, rumble
We ran away as quickly as possible
Because if we didn't we might have to go to the hospital
We got far, far away
And stopped when we reached a waterway
But just as we stopped I realised my sister was still at the mountaintop.

Olivia Kerr (9)
Fox Covert Primary School, Edinburgh

Foods And Fun

Arriving there in the middle of the night
Was a wonderful, shocking fright
When all the burgers were waving hello
In my head, I was thinking whoa

Lollipops showing me all around
Seeing marshmallows getting thrown on the ground
Shrimps taking a dip in a bubbly sauce
The broccoli were shouting, "I am the boss"

Flying up on a cotton candy cloud
Up at the top, there was a massive crowd
King Pizza shouting out commands
Trying to tell them some monsters are made out of sand

When everyone heard the frightful news
They all thought they would get a bruise
Chicken wings grabbing their spears
Out of the blue the fearsome beasts appear

It looks like a scary fight
In the end, it was all a night
I couldn't help myself, I took a bite
When I woke up I had a fizzy Sprite.

Rohan Bullock (11)
Fox Covert Primary School, Edinburgh

The Perfect Nightmare

Last night I had a dream
It would seem a lovely dream
But it was one to make you scream
It had cotton candy, chocolate fountains and toffee houses
And women wearing airhead blouses.

A queen it seems in a cotton candy dress
And girls in butterscotch dresses came up to say,
"Follow our lead"
Of course, I followed 'indeed'
They led me to a gingerbread castle.

It is wonderful
Suddenly a hand pulls me towards the forest no longer colourful
Sinister instead
The so-called Queen of the Forest said, "I wish you dead!"

She pulled out a knife
And called her wife
"Cook them in a pie!
Today you shall die!"

She lifted her knife
And I was ready to give up my life
But my eyes lifted
And I was home and the queens never existed.

Hannah Winton (10)
Fox Covert Primary School, Edinburgh

Axo Stadium

In my head when I am lying in my bed
Axo Stadium is waiting for me
I have a bed and a trendy racing game
It's really not that lame

Cute axolotls sitting in the nice clean seats
With little cup holders and a waterfall down at their feet
And a little guy selling hot dogs
And a little axolotl doing blogs

Vroom, vroom the cars went
As I sat in my tent
With a bed
That is really red
There's a few other things
Lots of banners and strings
A plane that drops tacos and pizza
Or maybe a hand heater
Don't forget water
I also have a pet otter
And he likes to dance
He's as fast as a cheetah
We play all day on video games

We love calling each other different names
Now the time's come to say goodbye
And have a lovely day.

Henry Haldane (10)
Fox Covert Primary School, Edinburgh

My Dream House

A house next to the deep big blue ocean
With lots of colour and emotion
Red walls like a Minecraft potion
A roof like a giant tortilla crisp

A roller coaster going *clink, clink, clink*
The cart is like a big bed going *clang, clang, clang*
Coming out of a hole in the house with a big bang
The roller coaster comes to a stop at the end

The PS5 jumping up and down
The walls white like a flat clown
The controller is a dog spinning round and round
Snacks and drinks line the walls on shelves

Seats going down to the screen
Walls very shiny and clean
The screen as big as a drilling machine
Movies play all day long

Rory Macdonald (10)
Fox Covert Primary School, Edinburgh

It's Not Real

One day, a bloke came to our house
Annoyingly, he awoke me from my slumber
Then I realised it was my brother
He awoke because my mother was divorcing my father

It was a pain, they were so inseparable
Miserable as it was I had to stay strong
I thought Mum was so wrong.
I was so sad but she said, "You'll never understand!"

Terrible as it was I could do nothing to change her mind
I couldn't find anything behind what happened
No one I could find made me feel happy
Anything kind immediately disappeared

I'm so mad, why did this happen?
I went to a salon and the trees danced in a lovely fashion
But whatever I try, it's all just so bad
I'm as sad as a water fountain, but it's not real!

Alice Costley (10)
Fox Covert Primary School, Edinburgh

You Score You Win

"If he scores, Scotland will be crowned champions of the world!"

Crowd chanting
Goalie distracting
Life flashing
It's now or never!

Country to glory
Write your own story
Obtain that trophy
Will you score?

Thinking of scoring
Whole country roaring
The rain is pouring
Come on just kick it in the goal!

The pitch is soaked through
Proudly wearing blue
You might achieve the goal you want to pursue
Come on you can do it!

Very, very tired
Feeling inspired

A goal is required
Time to shoot!

Goooooaaaaaalllllll!
Scotland win the 2044 World Cup!
For the first time in history
Scotland are bringing home the World Cup trophy!

Lucas Grant (10)
Fox Covert Primary School, Edinburgh

The Unicorns' Party

I yawn and stretch on my bed
Thinking of what was going on inside my head
I opened my eyes, I was in some sort of chocolate house
Wearing a sparkling golden blouse

There were unicorns, fairies and wizards there
Even a great big grizzly bear
The pink fluffy unicorns were dancing on rainbows
Sweets were flying out of volcanos

Chocolate was dripping out of the windows
All the fairies were dancing with their pink bows
The rainbow disco ball was glistening in the light
The wizards' wands were brown and bright

All of a sudden my eyes opened wide
I looked around the room and then I sighed
Oh no, I thought in my head, it was just a dream
No more unicorns sparkling with gleam.

Casey-Rose Mitchell (10)
Fox Covert Primary School, Edinburgh

The Magic Potion

I open my eyes to starry skies
As a rainbow-haired unicorn lies
I reach out to pet its fluffy mane
I feel my head spinning and my brain

I lie on a sweet cotton candy cloud
I feel glorious and so, so proud
All of a sudden while I'm relaxing wizards appear
With smiling faces and wonderful cheer.

Their wands glow so bright
In the darkness of the night
One of the wizards shoves her hand into their pocket
And pulls out a small glass bottle in the shape of a rocket.

"What that?" I wonder clearing my throat
"It's a magic potion that makes you float."
Without hesitation, I drink it
And open my eyes to the fairy lights in my room that are lit.

Abby Boyack (10)
Fox Covert Primary School, Edinburgh

Golden Ticket

My mum tucks me in saying, "Good night"
My eyes looking up, my eyesight turns white
My eyes drift away
I was on my way

My life flashed before my eyes
And out of nowhere a surprise
A man jumps out in a disguise
Willy Wonka appears with a prize

"Golden ticket!" A chance right here
"Any volunteers?"
For an infinite amount of chocolate for a year
"Yeah me, right here!"

It's nearly time to wake
I can feel my feet wobble and shake
Sorry but I have to say bye
I started to yelp and cry

I'm never going to believe
That it is the time to leave
"You can't leave!"
This is the place to achieve!

Emily M (10)
Fox Covert Primary School, Edinburgh

Nightmare

Nightmares terrify me through the night
When the lights are off it gives me a fright
Through the night I lay in bed
All I thought of was a dread

In my nightmare, the crazy Mad Hatter appears
With Voldemort close behind, I raged in fear
As my nightmare continues
My heart discontinued

A creature appears
With a long-headed beard
Bats form with a big pack
They flap as a witch clapped

As I turned there was a blizzard
That looked like a dancing lizard
There was ice that danced
I thought they laughed

Then I woke up from my sleep
And I said a loud weep!
Next time instead of being unprepared
I will be prepared!

Awa Jallow (10)
Fox Covert Primary School, Edinburgh

A Space Dream

Once I had a space dream
I was quite a bit scared
I was on the moon
Having tea with a polar bear.

Suddenly I saw an astronaut
But a giant frog caught him in its tongue
I started to run for my life
Before the frog could catch me in its wicked tongue.

He said, "Let me eat you, little boy,"
So I ran and ran to make him follow.
He started to slow down as he got very tired
But I went faster so he would not follow.

I ran to see something was waiting for me
It was a rocket ship as shiny as can be
I jumped inside the rocket ship
But at that moment I woke up to see it was just another silly dream.

Luke Jenkinson (10)
Fox Covert Primary School, Edinburgh

Dream Land Show

In my head
In my bed
My dream is waiting for me
The first thing I see are animals all around me
The first thing I will be is what I always wanted to be
It is that I can talk to animals
Out of the corner, I saw a key
I wondered what it was for, I looked but no one was looking for it
But I didn't see the letter on the ground
I decided to pick it up
When I opened it it was missing a bit
It said 'go to the spooky house', I sat with it to think
It took me a blink
To get there
There was a bear!
The bear saw me
I decided to run and the bear lost me, scary fun
I really need to go.

Alba Maiden (10)
Fox Covert Primary School, Edinburgh

The Paradise Beyond My Dreams...

As I settled down to bed
I felt as if I was dead
I lay in a heap
As I drifted off to sleep

Then I found myself in a paradise
With pools and cocktails as cool as ice
I felt that I was in a dream
But I could even feel the sun's beam

As I was relaxing on a beach
I heard a screech
Of someone saying run
And I knew this was my fun done

I looked behind me
And this is what I could see
A giant volcano erupting lava
Now this was the start of the drama

Suddenly I awoke
And I thought the dream had been a joke

But then I found a bit of sand
Lying in the palm of my hand!

Cora McRitchie (10)
Fox Covert Primary School, Edinburgh

When I Grow Up

I woke up, rose up
Reality took full control
Found out it was just a dream
I look out the window
Turns out I am
In Hollywood, California

And I have to go to work
I'm an actor
On that day I had a role
For a new movie.
I was as happy as a monkey

I saw a giant set
With a director shouting things like action, cut and that's a rap.

But then as I awoke my dream faded away back into the air
I dashed down the stairs like a cheetah.

"Mum, Dad I had the craziest dream last night."
"What is it, son?"
"Oh, it doesn't really matter."

Archie Fraser (10)
Fox Covert Primary School, Edinburgh

It Was All A Dream

Straight when I wake up, there's my friend Bob
He looks like a giant blob
He pulled me out the window to go fly
I could see the policeman floating so high

There was a walking bun
Also a big dog and a milk sun
The flying buildings were so amazing
The roller coaster left our hands raising

Bob said, "Let's go to New York"
When we got there I saw a fighting fork
There was acid rain
It made me feel some pain

I woke up and I was sad
My dad said, "Don't get so mad"
I wanted to let out a scream
The reason was it was all a dream.

Theo Daly (10)
Fox Covert Primary School, Edinburgh

Once Upon A Dream

What's inside my head when I'm lying in my bed?
Dreams, nightmares who knows what it will be?
There is a Starbucks next to Primark so let's go get a cup of tea.
Let's go on in and let the fun begin.
These matching sets are so cute!

But what if shadows come out at night?
Clowns in my imagination.
In the dead of the night, you might get a fright,
In my sight, there is only a bit of light.
But what if a ginormous tarantula comes to sleep on me?

Good dreams, dreams that are good and positive.
Bad dreams, dreams that aren't the best.

Ella Miller (11)
Fox Covert Primary School, Edinburgh

Nightmare

Last night I had a dream night,
All I can see are dark places,
Nothing has prepared me for this strange face,
I take a step forward with care.

As I glance left and right saying to myself,
"How did I get here?"
I hear something
Moving around.

Nightmare comes and fills your head with dread
They say, "It's not true, there
Is no point in fighting."

A wide grin spreads across its curious face
Running like it's in a race
I close my own in dread
Suddenly I wake up to find
I am safe at home in bed.

Zahraa Al-Behadili (10)
Fox Covert Primary School, Edinburgh

Night-Time At School

This is what a perfect dream would be
Close your eyes and you will see

Running down the hallway
It will be okay

Foxes coming in at night
I hope they don't bite

Swing on the monkey bars
Laughing like a racing car

School doors opening
It's the janitor Mr Orr

Me and the foxes hiding behind the door
Hiding on the floor

The children coming in for the day
The teacher coming for the pay

Time flies by in school
But does it rule?

Maybe not at night.

Edward Quinn (11)
Fox Covert Primary School, Edinburgh

Candy Land

In my bed,
In my head,
Candyland is waiting for me

A long sausage dog with a crown on his head,
The shiny flag is the colour red.
The cotton candy comes from the sky,
The giraffe's neck is very high.

The sloth sleeps quietly on a tree,
In my dreams, he's close to me.
Next, it's a unicorn with a horn on her head,
I think about her when I'm in my bed.

I love to dream every night,
My dreams end when it's light.
Thoughts take over in my head,
I can't wait to get back to bed.

Lylah Gilchrist (10)
Fox Covert Primary School, Edinburgh

Guinea Pig Golf

Tee-off
It's guinea pig golf
It's me v Honey here
It's not near

Losing bad
Really sad
Tied - feelin' alright
It's a good night

Family chanting
Very distracting
Honey leading
Game proceeding

Losing on the last
Feeling outclassed
It's neck and neck
Honey's in a wreck

Yes!
Honey's in a mess
Missed
A big twist

This to win
It's in
The Guinea Pig Shield
As shiny as gold is revealed.

Luke MacKenzie (10)
Fox Covert Primary School, Edinburgh

Candy Land

In the candy dream
There was a deer waiting for them it would seem
Panda enjoys eating bamboo and loves hugs
The turtle lays eggs under the sand and dug

There is a unicorn and it has a rainbow horn
And they are eating my front candy lawn
And the funny dog sat eating a giant bone
Then I made some cotton candy alone

A candy rainbow made of rainbow string
And a cherry tree swing
Now it's time to end the candy dream
But just before I go, I will take a bite of cream!

Iona Taylor-Bell (10)
Fox Covert Primary School, Edinburgh

Space

I was floating in space, beside me
Debris floated free
All of a sudden in a flashy light
Beside me, my shy dog, Doge.

I saw a giant T-rex dancing perplexed
Me and Doge went closer to inspect
I said hello, so did it
Astonished I asked where this place was.

It pointed to a planet
So me and Doge went closer and closer
It was covered in trees
Something rustled and I woke up.

Harris Lauchlan (11)
Fox Covert Primary School, Edinburgh

Last Night's Dream

I was eating ice cream
Then I dozed off into a dream

When I was a kid
I made a bid

And lost all my money
To a bunny

My mum thought it was funny
And gave me more money

This time I played poker
With the Joker

Next time I made a bet
On roulette

I put money on red
Then went to bed.

Aaron Gault (11)
Fox Covert Primary School, Edinburgh

Avoiding Space

I awoke and saw some unusual things,
Like some funny incredible dinosaur wings.

I awoke once more
Awoke again
A broken meteor chasing men.

Seeing a watchdog chasing after me
I find darkness all around me to see
A spark or was it a shark?
I counted 1, 2, 3.

Mark Rusakov (10)
Fox Covert Primary School, Edinburgh

My Life In A Dream

In my dreams, I wish for a life
To stay in a book
To crawl into some cosy nook.
I wish that I had some friends
I wish that they could stay until the end.
The dawn could raise me up
The sunset could set me down to sleep
But the mountains can't take the moon away
And the clouds can't take the sun away.
The wind can't stop my happiness
The rain can't stop my fun
Don't stop me now, or you'll regret what you've done.
Stop me now and you'll think you're a villain,
Stop me now and you will become a thief.
I recommend not to mess with me
Just leave me be.
Mountains are beautiful, so is the sunset that rises everything.
This is how I sleep,
This is how I live.
Someone's made me happy, someone's made me sad
But I don't let them put me down,
Just let them wake me up to a happy day.

In my dreams, I wish for a life
To stay inside a book
To crawl into a cosy nook.

Harriet (10)
Higher Lane Primary School, Manchester

My Luna

Once, in a dream, I was in a park.
I didn't know my surroundings.
It was just so, so dark.
On my left was an ice skating rink
And somewhere I heard a familiar *clink!*
I spun around. "What was that?"
A sigh of relief,
It was my cat.
It was then I saw the stranger's eyes.
Bloodshot, lonely and so, so wise.
Wait! I thought. Something was amiss
As I heard Luna's aggressive hiss.
Shaking, I gritted my teeth
As the stranger with large claws made a lunge at me.
As I awoke I was in my bed,
I felt dizzy. I bumped my head.
A downstairs voice I heard, it said,
"Wake up, you sleepy head!"
As I turned on my pillow, I saw my Luna.
Tired, soft and oh so mellow.
As everyday chaos starts in God's palm,
I wondered for the life of me, how was she so calm?
She lay, flopped on her side, her tiny paws splayed

Left and right
As she had left it there all night.

Priya (10)
Higher Lane Primary School, Manchester

The Tiny Little Dandelion

In a big, large forest, I slept under a tree,
A tiny little dandelion made me sneeze.
"Achoo!" I said and wiped my nose,
A unicorn said, "I hope that dandelion grows!
A problem it is, a nuisance you see,
It's always causing trouble for you and me."
And so I set out to find the Golden River,
Its magical ways, its beautiful shimmer.
To make my dandelion grow and grow,
I have to find its gleaming glow.
So we have to find a nutritious river,
But be careful of foxes or they'll have you for dinner.
Be their friend, although they're mean,
And they will show you the secret scene,
And so I found the magical river and stole a drop or two,
I sprinkled it on my little dandelion and so it grew and grew.

Inaaya Ishaq (7)
Higher Lane Primary School, Manchester

Climate Change

Ice is crashing into the sea
Because of things done by you and me
Penguins can't find enough to eat
Too many cars in the street
Monkeys with nowhere to live any more
Trees come crashing to the floor
Places where it never rains
People starving, hunger pains
Animals dying every day
Stop throwing rubbish away!
Too much pollution in the air
It's about time we took more care.

Time to take the bus to school
Keep the penguins nice and cool
Leave the trees where they are at
Monkeys happy in their habitat
Give some water to the poor
So the crops can grow some more
Re-use the bottle, don't throw it away
Animals live another day
It is possible if we change today
All the animals shout, "Hooray!"

Oliver Ware (9)
Higher Lane Primary School, Manchester

When The Stars Dance

When the stars dance
When the moon beams down
A small island appears at sundown
Creatures come from a blossom tree
And some come out from the rippling sea
Somewhere on the island is a special plant
Called the Gleamdream Flower which can enchant
The moon beamed its light to the hidden beauty
They searched up and down for the plant
Then they saw some sort of transplant
As a giant flower reached out from the centre of the island
Which could be seen from the highland
The animals jumped up and down, overjoyed
Then as quick as an asteroid
They snatched one of its leaves
Then the party began
As they all lay down, facing the stars
They looked at the stars
They watched the stars
They watched the stars dance.

Mila Pearson (10)
Higher Lane Primary School, Manchester

Got To Score

Dedicated to my mum

C elebration in my mind - the net is un-secure,
O ne quick dash - in a flash - I know I can score,
R ight up to the front but, alas, no more,
I trip and slither, ungraciously, onto the floor
N ever have I been so mad,
N ever have I been so sad,
E nd of game may be supposed,

C orrection! I remain composed
A mazingly!
M y strength perhaps a little slower,
P ulls me up and stirs my soul,
B ack goes my leg with massive power,
E xplodes my kick to reach its goal,
L oud cheers and shrieks fill my head,
L egend. Oh no! I wake to find I'm still in bed!

Gerry Campbell (9)
Higher Lane Primary School, Manchester

My Dream Come True

Will my dreams take me far
Or shoot off like a shooting star?
I see unicorns with sparkling manes
And magical mermaids with excellent braids
Naughty elves dance whilst reindeer prance
I see the magic flow as it all glows
I wish I could visit this magical place
As it is all over the place
The lush green grass and the crisp warm breeze
Are always how the weather seems
I dream this dream every night
But I wonder if there is any fright?
I see this picture start to freeze
As it moves on with the breeze
Then I find myself in bed just lying down on my head.

Phoebe Liu (8)
Higher Lane Primary School, Manchester

The Royal King

Every day I go to sleep
I dream about being a royal king
Give orders
Getting limousines here and there.
People always crowd me but I say no to the people,
Because they are not beautiful enough for me.
A walk in the park.
I see someone beautiful walk in the same park as me.
I ask to meet them in my castle.
Me and her became best friends.
One day, I asked her to marry me and she said yes.
We have four kids. Two boys and two girls.
Our children become kings and queens and live with the family name.

Oded (10)
Higher Lane Primary School, Manchester

Beauty Sleep

B eds to sleep in at night,
E ntering a new world that's bright.
A nd a place of fun,
U nder clouds of candyfloss, where I can skip or run.
T rees made of sweets, chocolate and gum,
Y outhful pleasure while I rest,

S leeping to make my mind and body its best,
L oving the glow of my skin
E very pleasant dream is a win,
E xiting this world of delight,
P arting with another lovely night.

Niamh Edney (11)
Higher Lane Primary School, Manchester

The Deep Underground

Once upon a time
There was a mysterious cold street

I hear engines and cars and
Stamping of feet

But I say to myself,
"What's under my feet?"

So let's go down underground
Where worms and beetles are all around

Deep underground is where I should stay
In the dark and the cold day after day

No sunlight where I am bound
Ancient artefacts waiting to be found

And centipedes dancing all around.

Hayden Newman (7)
Higher Lane Primary School, Manchester

All Over The World

Every night I dream of the same thing.
I can fly
I can fly across the world.
I try new foods, meet new people and go wherever I want.
First, I go to London and pretend to be the queen.
Then, I go to Paris and try every kind of cheese.
Now to Japan, to learn some Japanese.
How great is the world? Everywhere I've been
Everyone I've met makes me feel amazing.
Well that's it for tonight.
I wonder where I'll go next...

Alexa Griffiths (11)
Higher Lane Primary School, Manchester

Dream Jobs

I could be a vet,
Or fly a jet.
I could be a doctor,
Or pilot a helicopter.

I could be a police officer,
And catch bad guys.
I could be a teacher,
And change kids' lives.

I could fight fires,
Or fix tyres.
I could be a scientist,
Or a green-fingered botanist.

I could be a dentist,
And look after people's teeth.
I could be a poet,
Don't I just know it!

Lily Boyd (9)
Higher Lane Primary School, Manchester

Me And My Cousin

Me and my cousin together
We're in a nice funfair

When we had a lot of run
Everywhere we could see so much fun

We had a ride on a tall coaster
All the kids shouting loud, "Faster, faster"
It became very windy on the ride
All the kids held the bar very tight

At the end, it stopped, we were dizzy
Our day was full of fun, easy-peasy.

Sophia Samaei (7)
Higher Lane Primary School, Manchester

Superhero Powers

One day, the town was okay until a superhero came,
But then something smelt wrong.
A fire was burning just like steaks.
Everyone was in fear,
Just like a scared deer.
Firefighters fought the fire,
It was too strong like a cheetah.
The superhero put the fire out,
She was faster than a line of lightning.
Everyone cheered forever and ever.

Ruby Hepburn (7)
Higher Lane Primary School, Manchester

Stories

There are stories, tales and horror too,
But the best of stories are made by me and you.
It can be about monsters, dragons or wizards too,
But the best of stories are made by me and you.
It can be about fairies, cyclops and aliens too,
But the best of stories are made by me and you.
It can be about witches, vampires or zombies too,
But the best of stories are made by me and you.

Matthew Pritchard (9)
Higher Lane Primary School, Manchester

The Blitz

Erupting from the plane,
The bomb is ready to go insane,
Whistles as they skydive through the air,
The people below are not ready for this scare,
As they descend from the clouds,
The whistle becomes louder and loud,
Making themself known, as it hits the ground,
The bomb is high-tempered and stays red-faced,
Before you know it, they explode with rage,
Now on the earth's crust, the buildings are devoured,
Who could stop them now? The bombs were overpowered,
The planes soar through the sky, people say their goodbyes,
Parents and children parted,
They don't know 'The Blitz' has started,
From days to weeks, bombs have been dropped,
The civilians wonder when will it stop,
After 56 days the bombing began to end,
The citizens wonder if the Axis is a foe or a friend.

Sherelle-Kay Ngah (11)
Holy Family RC Primary School, Oldham

A World Of Destruction

People suffering,
Losing their mind,
What other mercy could they find?
Like destruction causing rubble,
All the trouble is doubled,
Warplanes dropping bombs,
As fierce as a lion's roar,
People bracing for safety,
Whilst mercy is currently being crazy,
Vengeance is being served to the poor below,
May they rest in peace,
As their hearts are feasted.
Being trapped in a different dimension,
While people are being captured in a state of depression,
The final bomb has been launched,
While the world is being torched,
This truly is a world of destruction.

Zina Aghaunor (10)
Holy Family RC Primary School, Oldham

Flying Chaos

Flying high in the sky,
People wondering why
Until it is time to say goodbye,
Remember the children who used to play?
Now they just sit there staring in rage,
Hoping they could go back to the olden days,
As the planes fly over with smiles on their face,
The civilians hide and take place,
The bomb has dropped,
Everyone has their doors locked,
The bomb starts whistling,
And everyone is listening,
The bomb hits the crust,
Everything has turned to dust...
Destroying everything in its wake,
People start to push and shove everything in their way.

Princess Manson (10)
Holy Family RC Primary School, Oldham

Nowhere Is Safe!

Erupting from the beast, creeping through the air,
Knowing what it's about to drop, is very unfair,
Lurking slowly behind its prisoners below,
Bursting into the clouds, with a row,
Making themselves known to the ants scurrying ahead,
Ready to destroy anything or anyone in its path,
While the kids were doing their maths,
Tigers emerged from the ground,
Ready to give London a great pound,
Children crying and soldiers dying,
The chuckling creating sculptures,
Into the earth's crust.

WWII.

Nathaniel Warburton (11)
Holy Family RC Primary School, Oldham

World War 2 Nightmare

Tiger 2 on the ground shooting like a madman,
Planes are dropping bombs, in a red-faced deadly pair,
Throwing sand like dirt in the air,
Ally shots are deflecting,
While the Tigers are detecting,
The Tiger's eyes open, he found a prey,
He had something to say,
I'm as strong as my name,
The prey turns pale, the Tigers get him tamed,
Clicking and clashing, small arms bounce,
The Tiger is panting, unable to pounce,
Overwhelmed, and cut down,
He gives his last howl.

Kacper Gorgosz (10)
Holy Family RC Primary School, Oldham

Bombs Falling Down To The Earth!

Bombs falling,
Erupting from the sky,
Like screeching banshees,
Down from the monsters up high,
Heaven says goodbye,
Skydiving through the clouds,
As the monsters shoot bombs,
Ready to kill souls,
As the wind blows,
Exploding the earth,
Making themselves known,
To the people all alone,
Running to their prey,
Faster and faster,
As they emerge to them,
Assembling to earth,
As they destroy the path.

Lilah-Rae Ward (10)
Holy Family RC Primary School, Oldham

Dream Death Of Battle

Planes are travelling through the sky,
Planes are looking for their victims,
Bombs are looking for their predator,
Bombing London and Manchester,
Send some guardians from above,
Children just sobbing their eyes out,
Where is the love?
Where is love?
The love,
The love,
Billeting officers taking children,
Parents are crying, not happy,
Children are going to the countryside,
Missing their parents, not overjoyed.

Joachim Osaigbovo (10)
Holy Family RC Primary School, Oldham

Nightmare In World War 2

Descending angrily, fiercely, through the smoke-fuelled sky.
Dropping evil bombs from up high!
Looking at victims from an eagle's height
Waiting to destroy everything in sight.
Creeping through the evil clouds,
Ready to destroy the gathering crowds!
The deafening sound of the hurtful destruction,
Let's pray for reconstruction.
Looking around at death and despair.
Hoping and wishing for this world to repair.

Ethan Shaw (10)
Holy Family RC Primary School, Oldham

Bombs Are Falling...

The bombs are falling,
Making an evil plan,
Chuckling to themselves,
As they skydive down,
To the innocent people below,
Scanning for their target,
Exploding at earth's crust,
Destroying homes,
Smashing pots and pans,
Like a monkey,
Arguing with people,
Devouring buildings,
Like a grenade,
Hitting the people,
As hard as a rock,
What will happen next?
No one knows.

Lexi-Mai Coop (10)
Holy Family RC Primary School, Oldham

A Nightmare Of Raining Danger

After stepping out of the air taxi,
The bomb slips through the clouds,
The unnoticed victims hear something in the sky,
Looking up, fright taking over them,
The bomb making its way down to the fascinating land,
Begins scanning for its enemy - and prey,
Dashing towards the hard concrete ground,
The bomb devours the earth.
Herds of people traumatised,
What have they just witnessed?

Jamison Hufton (11)
Holy Family RC Primary School, Oldham

Demons Flying

Demons flying whilst crying,
Knowing that many people will be dying,
Singing tunes whilst dashing through the sky,
People dying and screaming, "Oh my!"
Buildings falling and smashing,
Whilst hundreds of planes are crashing,
Planes causing roars, like boars,
Destruction all below,
Slowly getting covered with snow,
Making themselves known to the civilians who survived.

Aariz Shakeel (10)
Holy Family RC Primary School, Oldham

The Destruction

Screeching through the air,
Scanning for their prey,
Who knew who would go up there,
Yet the Blitz, who wouldn't care,
Erupting from the sky,
Creeping to kill souls,
While crunching on dead skulls,
The bombs will still explode,
Letting them know war is heading towards them,
Ready to destroy everything in their path,
Yet Britain won't let them pass.

Madison Ward (10)
Holy Family RC Primary School, Oldham

Evacuation Nightmare

The train station is a hectic shop on a Sunday afternoon,
Busy, noisy, scary.
Tears are overflowing, flooding the city,
Gas masks - rubber face-prisons - packages of hope,
Carried on the shoulders of every child,
Parents are bulls, huffing and puffing,
Grieving the loss of their babies,
As they drag their suitcases,
Dead weights, too heavy for little hands.

Kamen Smith (11)
Holy Family RC Primary School, Oldham

Destruction Deck Nightmare

Entering our territory,
Refusing to say sorry,
Swift like a ninja,
The flying body of destruction collapses onto the area,
Crashing and splashing,
The planes start smashing,
Hitting all in their lane,
Slowly losing their brains,
I'm petrified, whilst they're satisfied,
Oh, the sharp pain of sorrow,
Knowing there won't be tomorrow.

Bernice Cardoso (10)
Holy Family RC Primary School, Oldham

The Tiger's Roar

It locates during the day,
It lurks through the night,
Giving people a real good fright,
As loud as an elephant,
It roars like a tiger,
Its red face shouts with anger,
A fifty-two tonne monster sprinting a good pace,
Before the impact, people embrace,
Bullets bounce, clash and clang,
But it was nothing like the tiger's amazing mighty roar.

Alexander Jones (10)
Holy Family RC Primary School, Oldham

Nightmare Tanks For Destruction

Soldiers flying up the ranks,
Tanks ready to wipe cities blank,
Jets dropping grenades,
Cities needing air raids,
Tanks causing destruction,
Germany causing eruption,
Planes quickly racing,
Victims below are bracing,
Tanks ready to deliver,
Humans will quiver,
When tanks deliver the final blow,
The Earth will no longer glow.

Henzo Da Silva (10)
Holy Family RC Primary School, Oldham

Nightmare In World War 2

Descending from the creeping predator,
Thrilling down in terror through the misty sky,
Spying on their miniature prey,
Skydiving to accomplish destruction,
Rummaging through the dark, evil clouds,
To round up their territory,
Travelling loudly through the air,
To make their presence known,
Ready to destroy anything in its path.

Charlton Saopa (10)
Holy Family RC Primary School, Oldham

Planes Overhead

Beware, beware,
For the planes overhead will give you a scare,
Watching like a hawk,
As they let out a mighty squawk,
A beast is unleashed,
Destroying the clouds with bubbling rage,
The people down below
Crammed into a shelter, as if it were a cage,
The monster is to blame,
For the people on the ground are going insane!

Iliana Kara (10)
Holy Family RC Primary School, Oldham

The Unleashed Bombs!

Bombs are falling,
Scanning the earth below,
Creating a life-or-death experience,
Bursting to seek civilians,
Ready to destroy anything and everything in their paths,
Like a wrecking ball falling from above,
Trampling down in terror
Devouring buildings
Erupting everything in their wake.

Scarlett Ordano (11)
Holy Family RC Primary School, Oldham

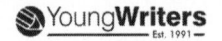

The Bombs Of The Blitz

The beast zooming through their sky,
Looking for their prey to devour,
The ants scurrying around on the ground,
After the beast releases its gas,
Breaking through the misty clouds,
Leaving a hole in the sky,
Bodies lying everywhere,
People crying in despair.

Corey Ashton-Barker (10)
Holy Family RC Primary School, Oldham

The Nightmare Battle

Interrupting the silence,
Creeping through the clear sky,
Searching for predators and prey to die,
Train stations packed like a bulging case,
People running at a fast pace,
Someone will save us, they believed,
As mothers and fathers grieved.

Kayla Ogbeide (10)
Holy Family RC Primary School, Oldham

Bombs Away

Scanning across the sky,
Travelling through the swooshing clouds,
Dropping onto the earth,
Leaving the atmosphere,
Causing destruction everywhere,
Ready to destroy more souls,
Some survived, some died,
Barely anything survived.

Connor McQuaide (10)
Holy Family RC Primary School, Oldham

The Blitz

Bombs are falling,
Exploding with rage,
Devouring our city,
Prey below, running for their lives,
Buildings collapsing,
Crush the people below,
For the impact, before bracing.

Rorey Tindall (10)
Holy Family RC Primary School, Oldham

William The Wicked Wolf

William the wicked wolf
Strong like a buffalo
And quick as an ostrich
A powerful jaw with a mighty bite
He fights in the woods every night
Locks his teeth and never lets go
You're going to die slow
Sharp teeth and claws
He likes to eat footballs
Howls with an owwwwwllll!

Aaron Devine (11)
Kirby Moor School, Brampton

Otters

Otters are my favourite animal
Their fur is as smooth as silk
Cuddly and cute
I love seeing them in the zoo
They're always in my dreams too.

Andrew Thompson (10)
Kirby Moor School, Brampton

In My Dreams...

In my dreams every night
A wolf flies with colours bright
Starlight roars making trees fall down
The dark shadow is making a frown
Running through the forest it starts getting cold

Here's where the story starts to be told
The wolf starts roaming the forest by day
Looking for his pup, who has gone astray
One frosty day he comes past a river, wide
There his pup lies inside.

Riley Fowler
Oak Wood Secondary School, Nuneaton

Nightmares

Creak!
The oak door broke open and a tall, mysterious figure crept in
He seemed dark and dangerous and I'm sure I've never met him
The blood-red beast looked like the walking dead
With its large, red body towering over me in my bed.

It had large, fierce horns made of lava
And razor-sharp claws that could cause grave drama
Its breath was hot and savage against my rosy cheeks
And now I wish I never woke up because of that eerie creak.

His fiery orange eyes glared at me with rage
And now I want to run away but I'm imprisoned in this cage
There is no escape, I must accept my fate
There is no escape, I am now this monster's bait.

Suddenly, I woke up, sweat dripping down my face
I guess there was no monster and there will be no murder case
And now I don't need to give a care
Because all of that was just a nightmare.

Benjamin O'Dea (9)
Tetherdown Primary School, Haringey

My Nightmares

In the darkest hour,
When the moon is high,
Nightmares awaken,
With a wicked sigh.

They slither and crawl,
In shadows unseen,
Whispering secrets,
In a voice so mean.

Their eyes like coals,
Burn with evil fire,
Haunting your dreams,
Fuelling your deepest desire.

They dance in the moonlight,
With eerie grace,
Taunting your sleep,
Leaving no trace.

Their laughter echoes,
A chilling sound,
Filling your heart
With terror profound.

They lurk in the corners,
Where darkness resides,
Feeding on fear,
As your sanity subsides.

The shadows grow deeper,
As the clock strikes three,
Nightmares emerge,
With the malevolent glee.

They whisper your name
In haunting refrain,
Beckoning you closer,
To their world of pain.

They play with your mind,
Like a crazy game,
Distorting life,
Driving you insane.

The walls close in,
Suffocating your breath,
A claustrophobic nightmare,
A dance with death.

Dread engulfs,
As reality starts to fray,

A distorted nightmare,
Leading you astray.

A chill wind howls,
Whispers of the undead,
Ghosts and ghouls,
Filling you with dread.

The veil between worlds,
Thin and tattered,
As worries emerge,
Sanity becomes shattered.

Heartbeats thunder,
Echoing through the dark,
The music of fear,
Leaving its mark.

Desperation grips,
As fair takes its toll,
A chilling song plays,
Consuming your soul.

The nightmares retreat,
As dawn light breaks,
Fading into shadows,
For all of our sakes.

Imagination soars,
Like a bird in flight,
Painting vibrant dreams,
In colours so bright.

Let your dreams take flight,
And remember in the darkness,
You hold the light.

Grace Lewis (10)
Tetherdown Primary School, Haringey

Dead End

I look up as the waves crash above me.
The white froth that engulfs the salty, turquoise water laughs at me, tauntingly.
The shore seems hundreds of miles away.
I scream!
Nobody hears.
Families frolic in the shallow end.
Why hadn't I listened?
What was going to happen to me?
Thrash, thrash, thrash!
A sharp ache pulses through my shivering body.
My lungs are on fire.
My head is as cold as an ice cube.
My eyes sting like nettles.
I kick my legs one last time, consuming all my remaining energy.
Ominous shadows dance beneath me and seaweed hooks onto my ankles like chains, dragging my thrashing body to the depths of this mighty sea.
Fish dart by like my hopes and dreams, all going to one place. Death!
Memories of my family swirl in my mind.
My eyes become filled with tears but each blink makes my body writhe in agony.

How long does it take for someone to drown?
How long does it take for someone to realise you're missing?
Are they looking for me right now?
I see my family in front of me.
I frantically swim towards them and hold my hand out.
My mum reaches out her hand too but I can't seem to grab onto it.
Gradually they disappear...
Why?
I beat my hands against my head.
I think over all the things I'll never be able to do:
I'll never be able to see Harry grow up,
I'll never be able to have my 13th birthday
And I'll never be able to see my dog again!
The thoughts rush through my mind,
Giving my body a sudden urge to try and swim up to the surface...
Push, push, push!
Will I make it...?

Flossie O'Dea (10)
Tetherdown Primary School, Haringey

Dreaming Lies

As I get into the house,
I answer all the nasty nonsense questions they ask me,
And of course, I answer with a lie.
I look out into the real world,
Whilst I wash my hands and see flying cars zooming through the bored street,
As the engine coughs and splutters.
Then my moaning mum starts shouting at me,
Why I haven't set the table?
And all I do is lie,
And I told her I was reading a fable.

After I set the table,
My brother comes with skaters on,
Skating to the table.
As we start to eat I think about how unfair it is that my brother is treated so much fairer:
The food I eat is disgusting, dirty slime,
Whilst my brother gets a fresh hot lasagne.
I am plastic and my brother is gold.
As I tell lies to my brother,
I look at him, his mouth widened from ear to ear;
His eyes sparkling with a deep sapphire blue light,
As blue as the ocean and his ears that spread to listen to my blabbermouth babble.

After finishing the food,
They ask me where I am going.
What am I going to do?
And bombard me with other inane questions.
You see...
The thing with me is that,
At the end of the day, I like to tell a lie...

Although, really this is all a dream inundated and thronged with lies.

My eyes opened to the bona fide, innocuous world.

Leo Konstantin (11)
Tetherdown Primary School, Haringey

Not So Little Red Riding Hood

Up the hill and over the lake,
There is an unknown mysterious place,
It is an old grand house,
With people whispering inside as quiet as a mouse,
When autumn comes around
And apples fall to the ground,
A strange girl is found,
Carrying a basket full of Brussels sprouts
And when she knocks on the door,
A wolf comes out,
Dressed in pyjamas and a dressing gown,
The wolf said, "Hello darling, why don't you come in and play?
Grandma's baked a lovely cake today."
The girl replied, "You see, I've brought some Brussels sprouts with me,
But could you bring the scissors for me, please?"
"Of course," he said
"But while I find, why don't you come inside?"
And when the wolf came back,
With some scissors and a coffee mug,
He said, "Why don't you come over here to give your old Grandma a hug?"

"Of course," she replied,
And the wolf beamed,
But when the girl gave him a hug,
She heard muffled screams,
So she cut the wolf's insides,
Only surprised to find,
That her real grandma was covered in filthy slime,
And with that, the wolf died,
Which to the grandma and the girl were happy to see,
As they had roasted wolf for their tea.

Paloma Lockwood (9)
Tetherdown Primary School, Haringey

The Night I Had A Dream

When you drift into the world of sleep,
Your brain is unconscious but your mind is deep.
You're transported to a magical land,
Your mind has something wonderful planned.

A land of mystery, a land of woe,
A land of yes, a land of no.
Your dreams burst and bubble eager to get out,
They play in your mind without a doubt.

Everything impossible can come true: unicorns, trolls and magic too.
Dreams swoop high; dreams love to soar,
Dreams flow gently, then majestically roar.
You shine as bright as galactic stars,
You drive in silver rocket cars.

Unfathomable powers,
Imagination flowers.
You are flowing around in the river of your dreams,
Nothing is what it seems.
You keep blissfully flowing,
Not aware of what comes next,
A nightmare!

Lightning strikes the skies,
You hear shrieks and cries,
Darkness looms like a monster and flies.
Good dreams retreat and roll their eyes,
"Help... no... get me out!"
There's no point to shout.
When things can't get worse,
When you feel cursed...

You are transported back to your bed,
You wake up and scratch your head.

You stare at the familiar wall,
And wonder if dreams even came at all.

Isabella Quirke (11)
Tetherdown Primary School, Haringey

Dreams

Dreams are wacky,
Dreams are weird,
You wake up in the morning,
Thinking you have a beard!

But sometimes they are frightening,
Sometimes they are scary.
Like you are being attacked by a witch,
Or an evil fairy!

Sometimes you are being chased
By a life-size mole,
Or sometimes you are falling
Down a never-ending hole!

But sometimes they are funny
As can be...
Like you are riding in a giant cup
Of English breakfast tea!

Or you are laughing about...
Who knows what?
And if you continue laughing,
It gets hotter than hot!

So now do you believe me,
About your crazy night song,
That streams in your head,
All night long?

Or is all you think you dream about
A screen of pitch black?
Well, in that case
I've got you a little hack.

Live crazy,
And do things weird,
And during the night,
Grow yourself a beard!

If you follow these steps,
And live your life strange,
You will wake up in the morning,
To a big surprising change!

Edie Hearn (10)
Tetherdown Primary School, Haringey

The Phoenix

My eyes shimmer like a ruby,
As flames come out of my mouth,
I fly at the speed of lightning,
My energy never runs out,
My voice is as loud as thunder,
As you see me in your nightmares,
Whoosh, the fire comes out,
Though I'm no imaginary creature,
I lurk in the shadows,
As I gobble up my suspect,
And try not to get into trouble,
My sparkling feathers glow in the dark,
As my treacherous ways get crueller,
I'm the source of light and know I'm getting stronger,
My screech is louder than a lion's roar,
And my claws are sharper than a dagger,
I'm the end of the world when the nights get longer,
I'm a death bringer
A horrible hater,
So be afraid,
Then suddenly I saw a light,
And heard a *thump, thump, thump*,
I felt the hard touch of a mysterious figure rapidly pulling me out of bed,

Then I heard a voice calling out to me,
"Hurry up, you're going to be late for school!"
Zara Zerdoudi (9)
Tetherdown Primary School, Haringey

My New Pet Dragon

Walking around a shopping high street,
I laid my eyes upon a pet shop.
Stepping into the shop,
My eyes could not comprehend what was at the back of the store:
A fire-breathing dragon with smoke coming out of its nose,
And its tail wagging like a windscreen wiper.
I begged the shopkeeper to buy it
But he never said yes...

I walked back home feeling demolished; but still had hope.
When I walked back to the shop, I demanded the dragon!
And I was surprised when he said yes!
Until he said, "I want a motorcycle in return for..."
Thanks to my luck I have seen a man selling one of them.
The shopkeeper sees the motorcycle with me and goes like a frog jumping in excitement!
Finally, as happily I and my lovely dragon united,
On the first test flight, we went in front of the Colosseum...

Like a knight on my dragon, I demanded him,
"Let out the flames here...!"

Aksel Akdogan (8)
Tetherdown Primary School, Haringey

Get Out Of Bed

In my dream,
I started to cry,
My mouth went dry,
I couldn't help but ask why,

When the sun set,
I began to frown,
All my happiness came crumbling down,

My head grew heavy,
My sight grew dim,
My hearing faded,
I felt jaded,

My heart froze,
My eyes closed,
That was the first time I sensed my foes,

I found myself in the year six corridor,
Panic set in,
I wanted no more,
Greek myths whispered on the walls,
Drowning out my frightened calls,

The door to my class creaked open,
My heart jumped, it felt broken,
There in the corner sat a mysterious creature,
I almost mistook him for my teacher,

His head turned,
My stomach churned,
Then all of a sudden he said,
"Wake up! Get out of bed!"

Theo Ogden (11)
Tetherdown Primary School, Haringey

My World

My world,
A place where I can go,
If I'm sad or if I'm tired,
Or maybe if I'm feeling low,
I just can't stay,
Oh, how I must go.

Maybe I've fallen out with a friend,
Or maybe I feel sick,
Even if I get annoyed, it's the place for me to go.

When I first landed there
I felt a nice sensation,
I knew just then that it had to be great,
So into the forest
With tangled trees,
I went in, without fear of any fleas!
5 seconds later I jumped out of that jungle,
And landed inside a magnificent tower,
Which seemed to have some sort of power.

My world,
It's beautiful, oh yes it is,

Old castles with ivy, rainforests with monkeys,
Oh, what a sight!
My world is surely the best for me!

Alma Lanzin Sohar (8)
Tetherdown Primary School, Haringey

The Breadboard

Let me tell you a dream that my daddy once had
I don't have dreams like his, mine are just bad
Everyone has flying dreams, but this one was different.
It was stupid, stupendous, silly, magnificent.
The dream started normally, he wanted a drink.
He went into the kitchen and up to the sink.
Next to the sink all covered in crumbs,
Was an old wooden breadboard that used to be Mum's.
He grabbed the old breadboard, adjusted his hair,
As quick as a flash, he flew up in the air.
He flew over homes, under bridges, and then,
Sped into London and up to Big Ben.
He went faster and faster on his tiny breadboard
You'll never forget how that piece of wood soared.

Max Davies (9)
Tetherdown Primary School, Haringey

My Faraway Land

There once was a world with sky as red as a rose,
The ground was as grey as smoke,
The luscious green grass was tickling my toes,
While I was chugging a Coke,
There was a wealthy man who lived on a cloud,
He was bowing to the world below,
"I'm going to help you all," he vowed,
To the lazy people all in a row,
He came to me and said something about a little man,
Who lived in a faraway land,
The little man whose name was Dan,
Was going to give us all a hand,
"A pound," declared Dan,
"For every step you walk,
To all the boys and girls,
Get off your bottoms,
And do some twirls,
Now let's get to work!"

Mack Lawrence (9)
Tetherdown Primary School, Haringey

Ammonite's Allure

Seashells, seashells, Milky Way,
Feathery friends, rummage and peck away,
In ancient seas, I danced and swayed,
A graceful spiral, in depth I stayed.

Seashells, seashells, Milky Way,
In whispered waves, my echoes play,
In a relic of oceans' past,
My form preserved, a treasure vast.

Seashells, seashells, Milky Way,
In a timeless tide, I used to sway,
I used to wander back and forth,
But now, I can only rest upon the shore.

Seashells, seashells, Milky Way,
In silent sands where memories lay,
A memory etched in stone's embrace,
A statement to time and space.

Cian Styles (10)
Tetherdown Primary School, Haringey

Once Upon A Futuristic Dream

I wake up in the sea.
The sea water is sweet, not salty just like my favourite popcorn.
I realise I have a watch that can control the weather.
I'm as relaxed as a sleeping sloth.
It is as sunny as the desert.
I see children whizzing around in jet packs.
I see billboards showcasing the iPhone 100 Pro Max.
It is so cool being in the year 5023.
I accidentally turn my watch to the thunderstorm setting.
Before I can change it back, I drop my watch in the sea!
The sky rains on me and I wake up screaming because I am so wet.

Alexander Pearce (8)
Tetherdown Primary School, Haringey

Land Of Dreams

Once upon a time
In a far, far place,
Where there is no crime
And people shout with grace,
Nothing will go wrong
All night long,
Well, come on,
Come and try
It won't make you cry
In this land full of dreams.

In this land full of dreams
There are lots of themes,
Like happy or sad,
Even angry and mad.
But either way,
You will feel glad.

In this land full of dreams,
In this place full of themes,
Are palaces covered in chalices.
When you're angry

You get candy,
And on the sea
You can ski.

Gabriel Vasiliou (9)
Tetherdown Primary School, Haringey

Darkness

Darkness creeps up on you
To scare you when you're feeling blue
It's all in your head
Like monsters under your bed
Just you and your mind
Once you have closed your blinds
An invisible ghost
Scares you the most
Eyes like flickering fire
As the creature rises higher
Creaking footsteps
Dusty spiderwebs

After what feels like an eternity
Daylight arrives in your dormitory
The wind whistles
Breakfast sizzles
Goodnight darkness although you are harmless
Hello morning.

Mei-Lei Lerman (10)
Tetherdown Primary School, Haringey

Drastic Dreams

Dreams only enter your mind at night
They set your imagination alight
Dreams creep and crawl all around your brain
And wrap you around an unbreakable chain

Dreams, well they come and go
However, they can make you overflow

They can fight, they can roar, they can even scream
But they could also be more evergreen
You can soar up high and set yourself free
As gliding birds fly above the sea
Climbing up a curling staircase with a jolly grin
It all ends when your eyes open to let the world in.

Nia Hadjinikolova (10)
Tetherdown Primary School, Haringey

Dreams Are A Surreal World

Dreams are a surreal world
That happens in your head.

Dreams are a surreal world
That finds you in your bed.

Dreams are a surreal world
That can be quite exciting.

Dreams are a surreal world
That can be quite frightening.

Dreams are a surreal world
That can't be controlled.

Dreams are a surreal world
That cannot be foretold.

Dreams are a surreal world
That we all love dearly.

Dreams are a surreal world
That we all love really.

B H (10)
Tetherdown Primary School, Haringey

Dream Journey

As swiftly as Neptune's winds,
My world transformed into a suspicious one,
My family and I were striding through a dense forest,
As I clenched onto a flying umbrella,
I was lifted yet a deadly owl swooped down,
As I returned safely to the rotting forest floor,
We reached a clearing that was as safe as a bedroom cupboard,
Calmly walking on for an age,
We eventually arrived at our ancient holiday cottage,
Out of a delicate, downstairs window,
Was a bustling city to welcome visitors.

Oscar Black (9)
Tetherdown Primary School, Haringey

I Had This Dream

I had this dream,
A very good dream
A miracle happened,
In this picnic.
A river of milk appeared to be.

I had this dream,
A field of flowers,
A pleasant smell
And I said, "What a beautiful life!"

I had this dream,
A flying angel, above the sky
Peaceful sunshine coming through the clouds
And I said, "What a beautiful life!"

I had this dream,
At the end of the day,
It's this planet that I really appreciate.

Warza Ahmed (9)
Tetherdown Primary School, Haringey

Dreams

Dreams creep up on you at night,
They dance into your sleep like a ballerina,
They slither into your mind as though a snake,
Some dreams are about a world of candy,
Others are like you being trapped in a cage with no way of getting out,
Dreams can scare you to death,
Or make you shout with joy,
Some dreams you just know they're dreams,
But others feel like they're very real,
Dreams come in all shapes and sizes,
You can never have too many dreams.

Esther Mitting (10)
Tetherdown Primary School, Haringey

What Are Dreams?

Dreams
They are like the weather.
They often shift and change with unexpected results
But when a storm comes
You don't just wake up with a snap
As for dreams when you are most afraid...
You enter the real world.
Relief.
Sunshine and a gentle breeze

What are dreams?
They are scary
They are pleasant
Long or short
Sometimes they are there,
Sometimes they aren't.

But they are always unusual and crazy.

Ben Cox (11)
Tetherdown Primary School, Haringey

One Dream

I have a dream that I will be a professional footballer.
I see a path to it.
As fast as a yellow, spotty cheetah!
As intelligent as my daddy!
Muscly like a roaring rhinoceros!
A quick eye like a soaring falcon!
Strong legs like my tiny, lovely sister when she kicks!
Agile like a determined, confident athlete
Forceful like a wrestler
Tranquil like my mummy and a translucent, stable tree.
Who knows maybe I will someday?

Zaki Copnall (8)
Tetherdown Primary School, Haringey

When I Went To Mars

Last night I took off in my super-turbo rocket blaster
Going faster, faster, faster, faster and faster
Until suddenly I landed on Mars with a kabam!
Out of my peephole, I saw an alien eating bread and jam
I jumped out of my rocket and said, "How do you do?"
The alien replied, "Blah de dah de moo."
I opened my eyes as my alarm clock was beeping
Thank goodness, I was just sleeping!

Emily Fox (9)
Tetherdown Primary School, Haringey

Nightmares

Stalking shadows creep up on me,
Danger lurks around every corner.

Fear isolates.

Pale fingers reach out
As I'm pinned helplessly.
Terror transforms my bones to stone.

A hurricane of horror whirls around me,
I am hurled upside down,
Tossed around,
Thrown into never-ending darkness.

For a moment, I don't know where I am.

But then
Daylight haunts me through the crack in the curtains.

I breathe - home again.

Annabel Bartlett (9)
Tetherdown Primary School, Haringey

The Golden Apple

The moment I saw it,
I grappled for the apple,
The creamy caramel
That dripped off the side of the apple
Made me cackle.
I immediately went to the chapel
So that you would buy me that golden apple.
But my mum said to buy me that glimmering apple would be a hassle,
I pleaded and pleaded until I finally got what I needed.
But I wasn't satisfied just yet,
I kind of wanted a pet!

Olivia Nilsson (10)
Tetherdown Primary School, Haringey

Once Upon A Lorax's Dream...

Green is grass,
Candy of trees,
Creature making,
Head scratching,
Film producing,
Thinking hard,
Mind wondering,
Imagination making,
Stories of land,
Dreams.
Land of Stories,
Making imagination,
Wondering mind,
Hard thinking,
Producing film,
Scratching head,
Making creatures,
Trees of candy,
Grass is green.

Amelia Farmer (9)
Tetherdown Primary School, Haringey

Dream Catcher

They come when you're in bed,
And plant themselves in your head.

The magic beans will start to grow,
Then your thoughts will squawk like a crow.

Some are of candyfloss dogs or chocolate bogs,
Some are of a football game or always the same.

Up in the sky sits the bean Hatcher,
And he is the one and only dream catcher.

Lottie Hilton (10)
Tetherdown Primary School, Haringey

My Hotel

In my dream, I own a hotel,
Where guests arrive and stay so well.
With beds like clouds and food so yummy,
My hotel is the place that's oh-so-comfy.

I will greet each guest with a friendly smile,
And make their stay worthwhile.
With hard work and care, I will earn my fee,
In my dream, that's how it will be.

Adriell Sitepu (8)
Tetherdown Primary School, Haringey

I've Got An Idea

I have an idea
Let me be clear
It's about a car
That doesn't go that far
It runs on carrots
And is driven by parrots
Turn the key and it roars
And opens its doors
Jump in to have fun
It's faster than you run
If you ask your mum
I'm sure you can come.

Zoe Brick (8)
Tetherdown Primary School, Haringey

Nightmares

Nightmares can be sad, scary and really hairy.
When they happen I am blocked
From the world but I still stay shocked.
Nightmares are the dreams you have,
However, they can be bad.
People may cry and they hopefully won't die
But in the end, all that nightmares are is your imagination.

Ben Schonfeld (10)
Tetherdown Primary School, Haringey

Dreams Beyond The Clouds

Upon the sky,
Angels above,
There came flying,
A little dove.
Left alone,
This is only a dream... or is it?
On a rainbow,
I shall sit,
Baking cakes,
With a colourful oven mitt,
My imagination grows,
I continue dreaming,
Isn't this an amazing feeling?

Sophie Bradstock-Smith (10)
Tetherdown Primary School, Haringey

The Jungle

Tall, swaying trees,
Long, lashing vines,
Terrific, terrifying tigers,
Magnificent, monstrous monkeys,
Vibrant, colourful fruit,
Luscious, green leaves,
Happy, joyful life,
Beautiful jungle.

George Towers (8)
Tetherdown Primary School, Haringey

Dreams

Dreams, dreams,
What are you?
You come and go,
You come at night and leave at day.
You are good, you are bad,
You are terrifying, perfect, beautiful.
I love you, I hate you.

Amelia Salgado (8)
Tetherdown Primary School, Haringey

Bison Dream

A kennings poem

Plains roamer
Grass grazer
Calf defender
Wolf charger
Prairie migrator
Natural wonder
Brave galloper
Shaggy protector

Bison.

Jackson Humphries (10)
Tetherdown Primary School, Haringey

Once Upon A Dream

D azzling ballerina.
R ustic, dusty mountains.
E legant little mice.
A mazing happy dreams.
M agnificent, sparkly jewels.

Emily Quirke (7)
Tetherdown Primary School, Haringey

Best Dream Ever About Football

In my dreams every night,
I kick a ball with all my might.
I'm just like Haaland shining bright,
Quickly turning left and right.
The grass is green beneath my feet,
I'm determined that I won't be beat.
But then Ronaldo tries to win the battle,
With a two-footed body slide tackle.

The whistle blows,
The crowd bellows.

I'm called forward for a final penalty,
I'm fearful as the spotlight's just on me.
The crowd falls silent all around me,
Then I score a screamer past the goalie.
The crowd goes wild when I lift the cup,
I hope for more but it is time to wake up!

Samuel Kirven (8)
The Richard Crosse (CE) Primary School, Kings Bromley

Elephants At Night

As I dream every night,
I do not know there is a magic flight.
I was watching the stars one special evening,
One star caught my eye because it was gleaming.
I realised that the star was an elephant,
It was obvious because it was flying so elegant.

Then the elephant swooped down,
It picked me up and did not frown.
It glided me away from my house,
It glided so quietly like a little mouse.
Luckily I had my teddy, Bhodi
I could tell that he was excited for the journey.

As I landed in a wonderland,
My mouth dropped onto Bhodi's hand.
Happily, he put it back up for me,
I could not believe what I could see...

Elephants dancing so happily and elephants eating off the joo-joo tree.
I danced and smiled and played with them
Could this place really be?
Majestic elephants were partying with me.

So when you see an elephant passing by,
It might just pick you up and fly.
So keep your eyes open every night
And maybe you will get a flight.
But when you find yourself in bed,
You will find elephants have left a special memory in your head.

Ava De Costa (8)
The Richard Crosse (CE) Primary School, Kings Bromley

Dancing On Moonlight

I am on stage and my heart beats fast,
As I see the theatre huge and vast,
Whilst the audience stares at me,
I feel as brave as I will ever be.
The music starts and I begin,
I dance on stage to hopefully win.
Dancing light as a beautiful feather,
Trying to make no terrible error.
I know the music off by heart,
My dance is like a piece of art.
The audience watches my every move,
While I follow every groove.
Now the song is at an end,
As I do my last bend.
The people stand and clap at me,
I feel as true as can be,
Not long ago I was a beginner,
But now I feel I am a true winner.

Eleanor Parry (9)
The Richard Crosse (CE) Primary School, Kings Bromley

YoungWriters®
Est. 1991

YOUNG WRITERS INFORMATION

We hope you have enjoyed reading this book – and that you will continue to in the coming years.

If you're a young writer who enjoys reading and creative writing, or the parent of an enthusiastic poet or story writer, do visit our website **www.youngwriters.co.uk**. Here you will find free competitions, workshops and games, as well as recommended reads, a poetry glossary and our blog.

If you would like to order further copies of this book, or any of our other titles, then please give us a call or visit **www.youngwriters.co.uk**.

Young Writers
Remus House
Coltsfoot Drive
Peterborough
PE2 9BF
(01733) 890066
info@youngwriters.co.uk

YoungWritersUK **YoungWritersCW**
youngwriterscw **youngwriterscw**